W9-AFZ-241

MY BROTHER'S BAR MITZVAH

written by
Janet Gallant

illustrated by
Susan Avishai

Kar-Ben Copies, Inc.

Rockville, MD

GLOSSARY

Bimah	*(Bee-ma)* - pulpit
Hanukkah	The Festival of Lights commemorating Jewish freedom
Kippah	Headcovering
Mazel Tov	Congratulations (literally, "good luck")
Minyan	Quorum of 10 for prayer
Shabbat	Jewish Sabbath (sundown Friday to sundown Saturday)
Torah	Five Books of Moses

Gallant, Janet.
   My brother's Bar Mitzvah / Janet Gallant; illustrated by Susan Avishai.
   p.   cm.
   Summary: Sarah is worried that her brother Ben, who still makes loud noises and messes, won't be ready for his Bar Mitzvah.
   ISBN 0-929371-20-8 (HC) — ISBN 0-929371-21-6 (pbk.)
   [1. Bar Mitzvah—Fiction. 2. Brothers and sisters—Fiction. 3. Jews—United States—Fiction.] I. Avishai, Susan, ill. II. Title.
PZ7.G13619My 1990
[E]—do20   90-4879
                                                                   CIP
                                                                   AC

Published by KAR-BEN COPIES, INC. Rockville, MD 1-800-4-KARBEN
Printed in the United States of America

To my husband, Andy.
                    —J.G.

For my Ben, who has come of age.
                    —S.A.

Grandma was the first to say it.

We were looking through her favorite photo album, the one with the pictures of my brother Ben and me. I love to do this with Grandma. She always tells funny stories.

"Here's a picture of you when you were learning to talk," she'll say. "You called your Mom 'Da-Da,' you called your brother 'Ma-Ma,' and you called your Dad 'Boo.' "

Then Grandma gave me a hug. "You and Ben are growing like bean sprouts," she said. "I can't believe it's only a year until Ben becomes a man."

I didn't understand.

"What do you mean?" I asked. She knew Ben was only twelve. Sometimes he acted even younger than I do, and I was only eight.

"Oh, Sarah," she said…"I was just thinking about Ben's Bar Mitzvah next fall."

I knew about the Bar Mitzvah. There would be a special ceremony at the synagogue when Ben turned thirteen. But what did that have to do with becoming a man?

I thought about my brother. "Big Bad Ben" I called him. He pulled bubble gum out of his mouth in long strings. He liked to sneak up and scare me with loud animal noises. Once he dropped my favorite music box that used to play "Clementine." Now it went *plip plunk pfft.* How could Ben become a man in just one year?

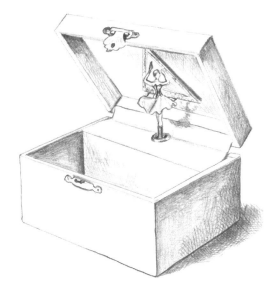

"Grandma," I said, shaking my head, "he'll never make it."

"Oh, yes he will," she said. "When he stands up in the synagogue to read from the Torah, he'll be a man. Just wait and see."

The next time someone said it was at our family Hanukkah party. The house was full of people. Mom was in the kitchen, piling doughnuts on a tray and talking to our neighbor, Mrs. Golden, about Ben's Bar Mitzvah. Again. Mom talked about it too much. She seemed to care a lot more about that Bar Mitzvah than she did about my bowling party last summer.

"Ben practices his Torah portion every night," Mom said. "He studies so hard."

"He should," said Mrs. Golden, "After all, he's almost a man."

What did she mean? Dad was a man. Grandpa was a man. Mr. Golden was a man. But Ben was a messy, dumb kid.

"How can he turn into a man so fast?" I asked Mom.

She laughed. She thinks a lot of things I say are funny even when I'm not trying.

"When Ben becomes a Bar Mitzvah," she explained," he'll be considered an adult member of the Jewish community. He will be able to read from the Torah, lead services, and be part of a minyan. So, we'll say that Ben is a man."

"But Mom," I said, "there's not enough time."

"Oh, he'll be ready," she said.

One night I heard Ben chanting Hebrew in his room. The sign on his door said PRIVATE KEEP OUT, but I always tried to trick my way in. First, I knocked.

"Who is it?" Ben asked.

"It's Sarah. I want to ask you a question."

He opened the door a crack.

"Do you have a Torah in there?" I asked.

He opened the door all the way. "No, silly. The Torah is in the synagogue."

"Then how do you learn your Bar Mitzvah part?"

"From a book. It has the same Hebrew words as the Torah, and the meaning of the words in English."

"Can I see? Please?"

It worked. He let me in. I looked at the heavy book he was studying. I also looked at his desk, his bed, and his floor. I saw pencils, last week's comics, baseball card wrappers, a cereal bowl, eraser dust, and dirty socks. I thought about Ben becoming a man.

"You'd better get to work," I told him.

That spring, Mom and Dad asked us to help with the Bar Mitzvah plans. All of our family and friends would be at the synagogue to celebrate with Ben, and after the service there'd be lunch for everyone.

"You mean Ben gets a ceremony AND a big party?" I asked.

"He does," said Mom.

"And cake?"

"Yes."

"And presents?"

"Yes."

"I'm having a Bar Mitzvah for my ninth birthday," I said.

Mom kissed me, and Dad gave me a hug. "I'm afraid you'll have to wait a few years. Then you'll have a Bat Mitzvah that will be every bit as special as Ben's Bar Mitzvah." It still wasn't fair, but I felt a little better.

We talked about what to serve at the Bar Mitzvah lunch.
Mom said, "Chicken."
Dad said, "Chicken."
I said, "Fried chicken."
Ben said, "Pizza."
That's not very grown up, I thought.

We all wanted music. Our whole family loves to dance and sing. Dad's friend is a folk dancer, so we decided to ask him to teach everybody Israeli dances. Ben said he hoped they could do a kid's dance that would go faster and faster until everybody got dizzy and fell on the floor.

That's not very grown up either, I thought. But it sounded like fun.

All summer I kept my eye on Ben, but I didn't see any changes. Before school started, Ben and I helped address the invitations. We mailed them to our relatives and neighbors and friends. Ben even invited his teachers.

Then Mom told Ben he had to go shopping for a Bar Mitzvah suit. Ben hates shopping.

"Why can't I wear my jacket from last year?" he asked.

"Because it doesn't fit," Mom said.

"So?" said Ben.

I was sure he wouldn't make it.

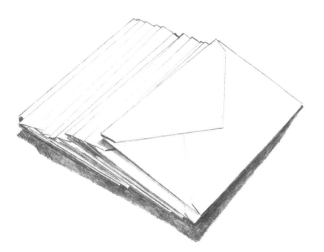

Finally it was Saturday morning, the day of Ben's Bar Mitzvah. Our house was full of people. Grandma and Grandpa were there, and so were two of my aunts, one uncle, and three cousins.

I rushed downstairs early to see Ben. It was his last chance. Had he changed overnight? No. He was the same old Ben, only nervous. I felt pretty bad. Even if he was Big Bad Ben, I didn't want his Bar Mitzvah ruined.

Mom and Dad didn't seem to notice that Ben was still a kid.

"We're so proud of you," Mom said, giving him a hug.

Dad put his arm around him. "This is a day you'll always feel good about."

I didn't think so.

When we got to the synagogue, I sat down between Grandma and Grandpa and waited for the service to begin. The door in the back of the sanctuary opened, and first the rabbi, then the cantor, Mom, Dad, and Ben walked up the aisle.

"He's so handsome in his new suit," Grandma whispered. Ben's hair was smoothed down under the silver kippah Grandpa had given him. He had a snowy white prayer shawl wrapped around his shoulders.

Was that really Ben?

Ben sat with Mom and Dad on the bimah. He didn't seem nervous anymore. When it was time for the Torah service, the rabbi opened the ark and took out the Torah. But instead of holding it himself, he gave it to Ben! It looked heavy, but Ben stood straight and held it up. I wasn't so worried anymore.

Mom and Dad took the silver ornaments and the cover off the Torah. Ben unrolled it. He chanted the blessings in a strong voice. Then he read from the Torah and told us what the Hebrew words meant.

"God created the world in six days," Ben said. "He blessed the seventh day and on that day He rested. Shabbat is our day for blessing and rest."

It was hard to believe that was my brother up there. He was just a kid, but he sounded like a rabbi. When he was done, the real rabbi stood and spoke. "Mazel Tov, Ben. Today, you've made your family and friends proud. You're a fine young man."

Everybody in the synagogue was smiling. Ben looked very happy. Maybe he hadn't turned into a grownup, but he'd done what grownups do.

"See," said Grandma. "Now he's a man."

This time I knew what she meant.